Sugar
COOKIES
Sweet Little Lessons on Love

written by
Amy Krouse
Rosenthal

illustrated by
Jane Dyer &
Brooke Dyer

HARPER
An Imprint of HarperCollinsPublishers

Sugar Cookies: Sweet Little Lessons on Love
Text copyright © 2009 by Amy Krouse Rosenthal
Illustrations copyright © 2009 by Jane Dyer and Brooke Dyer
Manufactured in China.

Library of Congress Cataloging-in-Publication Data
Rosenthal, Amy Krouse.
Sugar cookies / written by Amy Krouse Rosenthal ; illustrated by Jane Dyer and Brooke Dyer. — 1st ed.
p. cm. — (Sweet little lessons on love)
Summary: Baking cookies teaches us many lessons about life and love.
ISBN 978-0-06-174072-5 (trade bdg.) — ISBN 978-0-06-174074-9 (lib. bdg.)
[1. Cookies—Fiction. 2. Baking—Fiction. 3. Love—Fiction. 4. Conduct of life—Fiction.] I. Dyer, Jane, ill.
II. Dyer, Brooke, ill. III. Title.
PZ7.R719445Su 2009   2008047703   [E]—dc22   CIP   AC

Typography by Rachel Zegar
09 10 11 12 13 SCP 10 9 8 7 6 5 4 3 2 1
❖
First Edition

Sister Love means if I ask you, Katie Krouse Froelich, to share your famous sugar cookie
recipe with the readers of this book, you say without hesitation, *it would be my pleasure.*

*When cooking, it is important to keep safety in mind. Children should always ask
permission from an adult before cooking and should be supervised by an adult in the
kitchen at all times. The publisher and author disclaim any liability from any injury that
might result from the use, proper or improper, of the recipe contained in this book.*

To Jason, the love of my life
—A.K.R.

For Sophie Petunia
—B.D. & J.D.

ENDEARMENT means,

Come here, my sugar, my cookie,

my sweet little morsel.

CONSIDERATE means,

I waited until you got home so we
could lick the bowl together.

HEARTFELT means,

I made these sprinkly cookies for you because
I know they're your absolute favorite kind.

COMPASSIONATE means

that when you burn the cookies to a crisp,

I'll be there to give you a hug.

ADMIRE means,

I really look up to you and the way you are with your cookies. You remind me of what is good and possible in this world.

FORGIVE means,

I needed some time to get over what you said about my cookies—'cause that wasn't very nice—but now I think I'm ready to play with you again.

SUPPORTIVE means

that when your cookies are a huge hit at the bake sale,

no one is happier for you than I am.

TENDERNESS means,

See how we're lifting the fresh cookies
from the tray with care and gentleness?
That's the same way we treat another's heart.

ADORE means,

I think you're simply delicious.
Oh, I could just gobble you up.

EXPANSIVE LOVE means,

I love this cookie, and

I love this cookie so much too, and wait,

I really love this cookie as well.

My love keeps growing to make
room for each new cookie.

CONSTRUCTIVE means

that if the cookie tastes funny, I'm going to be honest and tell you.

I think you mixed up the
salt and sugar, sweetie.

UNCONDITIONALLY means
that even when you mess up the cookies,
my love for you doesn't change one single bit.

UNREQUITED means,

He sure loves her cookies, but I don't think she feels the same way about his cookies . . . or maybe she just hasn't noticed them yet.

REQUITED means,

Look!

They both love each other's cookies!

CONNECTED means,

We're making these cookies together so naturally and easily,

like we somehow know exactly what the other is doing

and what needs to be done next.

HEARTBROKEN means,

My heart feels sad and hurt, like a crumbling cookie.

TRUE LOVE means,

I like a lot of cookies, but this cookie here,

this cookie is extra-special. . . .

My love for it is pure and rich and endless.

SELFLESS means,

No, really, please,

I want you to have the last cookie.

BLISS means,

Oh my, the aroma! The divine taste!

I'm in total cookie heaven.

CHERISH means

that there is nowhere in the universe I'd rather be than

here in our kitchen, baking sugar cookies with you.

PROTECT means,

I will always be here to keep your cookies safe.

HOW MUCH I LOVE YOU means
that even if I made cookies from morning to night every single day
forever and ever and ever, it still wouldn't even come close.

Sugar
COOKIES

INGREDIENTS

½ stick butter

¾ cup sugar

2 eggs

1 teaspoon vanilla

2 cups all-purpose flour

½ teaspoon baking soda

frosting

sugar for sprinkling

DIRECTIONS

Combine sugar and butter, and mix well. In a separate bowl, combine eggs, flour, vanilla, and baking soda. Mix into the butter mixture and chill dough for one hour.

Roll out dough into small balls and place onto ungreased cookie sheet. Bake for 8–10 minutes at 350 °F.

Let the cookies cool completely, and then frost.

Sprinkle with sugar.